CYCLING
LANCE ARMSTRONG'S IMPOSSIBLE RIDE

by Michael Sandler

Consultant: Happy Freedman
Coach, Columbia University Cycling and
Faculty, Serotta School for Cycling Ergonomics

BEARPORT
PUBLISHING COMPANY, INC.

New York, New York

Credits

Editorial development by Judy Nayer

Cover and title page, Doug Pensinger/Allsport/Getty Images; Page 4-5, Doug Pensinger/Allsport/Getty Images; 5 (inset), Andreas Rentz/Bongarts/Getty Images; 6, AP/Wide World Photos; 7, Joe LeMonnier; 8-9 (both), Linda Armstrong Kelly/Sports Illustrated; 10, Stephen Dunn/Getty Images; 11, Linda Armstrong Kelly/Sports Illustrated; 12, GrahamWatson.com; 13, Linda Armstrong Kelly/Sports Illustrated; 14-15, ©Eric Gaillard/ Reuters/Corbis; 15 (center), AP/Wide World Photos; 16, AP/Wide World Photos; 17, ANJA NIEDRINGHAUS/ AFP/Getty Images; 18, Allsport UK/ALLSPORT/Getty Images; 19, AP/Wide World Photos; 20-21 (both), Linda Armstrong Kelly/Sports Illustrated; 22, MICHAL SVACEK/AFP/Getty Images; 23, Joe Raedle/Newsmakers/ Getty Images; 24, JOEL SAGET/AFP/Getty Images; 25, Tom Able Green/ALLSPORT/ Getty Images; 26, JAVIER SORIANO/AFP/Getty Images; 27, AP/Wide World Photos; 29, AP/Wide World Photos.

Design and production by
Ralph Cosentino

Library of Congress Cataloging-in-Publication Data

Sandler, Michael.
  Cycling : Lance Armstrong's impossible ride / by Michael Sandler.
      p. cm. — (Upsets & comebacks)
  Includes bibliographical references and index.
  ISBN-13: 978-1-59716-167-1 (library binding)
  ISBN-10: 1-59716-167-5 (library binding)
  ISBN-13: 978-1-59716-193-0 (pbk.)
  ISBN-10: 1-59716-193-4 (pbk.)
  1. Armstrong, Lance—Juvenile literature. 2. Cyclists—United States—Biography—Juvenile literature. 3. Bicycle racing—Juvenile literature. I. Title.

  GV1051.A76S26 2006
  796.6'2092—dc22

                        2005026088

For more information, write to Bearport Publishing Company, Inc., 101 Fifth Avenue, Suite 6R, New York, New York 10003. Printed in the United States of America.

10 9 8 7 6 5 4 3 2

Table of Contents

The Race of His Life

Could Lance Armstrong make it back? Once he had been a champion cyclist. He was known for his blazing speed and unbreakable **will**. Then he lost almost everything. He lost race after race. He lost his famous strength and speed. He nearly lost his life!

Lance Armstrong during the 1999 Tour de France

No athlete had ever come back from a downfall like this to return to the top of his sport. Yes, Lance had won some races, but not the **Tour de France**! Every great cyclist in the world would be fighting him for the trophy.

Lance pushed down on the pedals of his bike. The race was on!

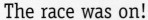 Bicycle races are won by completing a course in the least amount of time.

The Tour de France

The Tour de France is cycling's most important race. It lasts almost a month. Each day's ride, called a stage, is just one part of the whole race. The next day, the race continues.

Riders cross the entire country of France. They travel through valleys. They speed through cities. They climb steep and **rugged** mountains.

Almost 200 cyclists begin the Tour de France. Often, only 150 or so riders finish.

The race is over 2,000 miles (3,219 km) long, but not everyone finishes. Many cyclists are forced to drop out. Some are injured. Some crash. Some simply quit, unable to handle the pain and **pressure**.

The Tour is long and dangerous. Winning it, however, is every cyclist's dream.

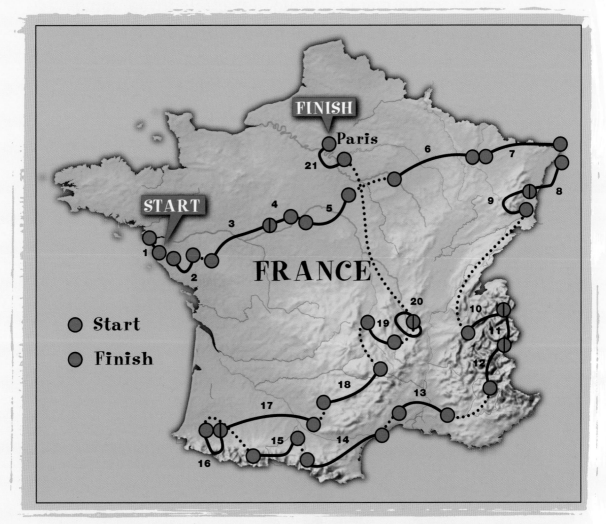

This is a map of the 21 stages of the 2005 Tour de France. The dotted lines indicate parts of the race that riders cannot travel over by bicycle.

A Boy and a Bike

Winning the Tour was Lance's dream. It had been for many years. Lance's mother, Linda, bought him his first bike when he was seven years old. He loved riding from the start. He loved zooming around his neighborhood in Plano, Texas. He loved going fast, and the scary thrill of **hurtling** down a hill.

As Lance grew older, he tried sports like football, basketball, and soccer. Somehow, they weren't as much fun as racing around on a bike.

Lance at age eight

By high school, Lance's mother was driving
him all over the state to **compete** in bike races.
More often than not, Lance came home the winner.

Lance during a
race at age 14.

Lance started bike
racing when he was
just 10 years old.

A Terrific Teen

Every day when school let out, Lance hopped on his bike to train. He rode through the city. He rode through the countryside. He took long rides by himself through the Texas hills. He grew stronger and faster, and began to dream of winning races like the Tour de France.

At races across Texas, Lance's speed caught everyone's attention. He took off like a rocket from the start. It was rare that anyone caught up to him.

Lance also loved the triathlon, a sport that combines running, cycling, and swimming.

The country's top cycling coaches also noticed Lance's amazing ability. In 1990, he was invited to try out for the U.S. national team.

Lance's hero is his mother. She raised Lance by herself, always struggling to make enough money to support them.

Hard Lessons

In Texas, Lance could win on speed alone. On the U.S. team, however, Lance would ride against tougher competition. At this level, winning required speed *and* **strategy**.

Lance's coach, Chris Carmichael, tried to teach Lance the secrets of cycling. He told Lance to start slow, to save his energy for the finish. Lance, however, preferred to burst into the lead. He didn't listen to Chris.

Lance and Chris Carmichael

Lance had to learn the hard way. At the 1990 **Amateur** World Championships, he stormed away from the pack of other riders. For three **laps**, he held the lead. Then his body shut down. Other racers caught up to him and easily sped by.

Lance finished in 11th place at the Amateur World Championships. Although he couldn't hold the lead, it was the best finish ever by an American rider.

Turning Pro

Lance decided it was time to listen to his coach. His racing improved. He began to win major races. In 1992, he was ready to turn **professional**.

Lance's first pro race was a long, hard ride in the mountains of Spain. The weather was awful. Bone-chilling rain drenched the riders. Many racers quit, scared by the rain-slick mountain roads. Lance kept going, but finished in last place.

In the 2004 Tour de France, Lance also faced rainy conditions.

It was a **depressing** first race. That night Lance thought about quitting. Then he changed his mind. *I didn't give up in the race*, he thought. *I'm not going to give up on cycling.*

When it rains, mountain roads become dangerous. Riders can fall off their bikes.

Going down a mountain, bike racers can reach speeds of 60 miles per hour (97 kph)— as fast as a car on a highway.

Reaching the Top

Lance's racing got better. Slowly but surely he was putting it all together—his amazing speed, his furious **determination**, and the strategies his coach had taught him.

Lance's finest moment yet came at the 1993 World Championships. At the time, Miguel Indurain (mee-GEHL IN-der-rayn), the blazing Spanish rider known as "Big Mig," was clearly the best cyclist in the world.

Lance crosses the finish line to win the 1993 World Championships.

On a steep hill near the end of the race, Lance went head-to-head with Big Mig. He pushed his body to the limit. He sped up the hill. He passed Big Mig and never looked back. Lance was champion of the world!

The winner of the World Championships gets to wear a rainbow-striped jersey in every race for the next year.

In 1993, at the age of 22, Lance raced the Tour de France for the first time. He won a stage, becoming the youngest rider ever to do so. Then he dropped out. The French mountains were just too tough.

In 1996, Lance set his sights on cycling's biggest prize. He dreamed of winning the mighty Tour de France.

The year before, Lance had finished the Tour for the first time. This year he wanted more. Yet Lance's dreams slipped away as soon as the Tour began. His legs ached. He didn't feel right. After just six stages, he quit. Quitting wasn't something that Lance usually did! What was wrong?

For months, Lance had aches and pains. One day, he started coughing up blood. When Lance went to the doctor, he couldn't believe what he was told: *You have cancer.*

Lance at the 1996 Olympics, a few months before he learned that he had cancer

Cancer is a deadly disease that kills almost 600,000 Americans each year.

A Race to Survive

Lance was terrified. He was so scared of dying. *Why me?* he thought. *I'm so young, just 25!*

Despite his fear, Lance couldn't give up. Beating cancer was a race to survive. He remembered how he fought the mountains in his first pro race. He would fight this disease the same way!

Lance leaned on his mother for support during his fight against cancer.

The doctors operated on Lance's body. They gave him painful **treatments**. Lance's hair fell out. He grew thin and weak.

One day he got on his bike. While riding up a hill, he watched ordinary riders speed past him. Only months before, he'd been the fastest cyclist in the world!

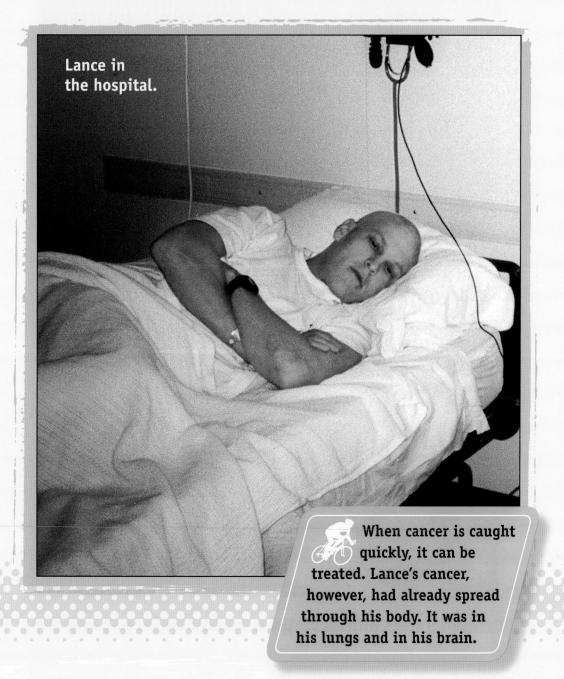

Lance in the hospital.

When cancer is caught quickly, it can be treated. Lance's cancer, however, had already spread through his body. It was in his lungs and in his brain.

Hoping for a Second Chance

For weeks, Lance waited nervously to find out if the treatments had worked. Had they killed the cancer? Finally, his doctors called. The cancer was gone! Lance had beaten the terrible disease.

Now he had a second chance at life. He wanted to race again. First, however, he had to get back in shape. Fighting cancer had taken away his strength.

Lance visits with cancer patients at a hospital in Prague.

It took months of training before Lance could return to competition. When he did, people were sure he wouldn't be the same rider as before. People were right, in a way. Lance wasn't the same. He was better.

Lance during a Ride for the Roses bike ride. This event raises money for the Lance Armstrong Foundation. The money goes to help cancer survivors.

Pro cyclists race for **individual** prizes, but they ride as parts of teams. During a race, teammates work together. Lance's old team dropped him while he was recovering from cancer. Before racing again, Lance had to find a new team.

Taking on the Tour

In 1999, Lance entered his first Tour de France since beating cancer. He burst out of the start like the old Lance, riding so fast that he broke Big Mig's speed record. Lance was in first place!

When he lost the lead after Stage 3, people thought Lance was fading. He wasn't. Beating cancer had made him smarter. He had finally learned Coach Carmichael's lesson—patience!

Lance during Stage 7 of the race.

Lance was **conserving** his strength until the time was right. In Stage 8, Lance broke away, zooming to the finish ahead of everyone else. For the next 12 stages, he never trailed again.

On July 25, 1999, Lance rode into Paris to claim his trophy. He was only the second American ever to win the race. Greg LeMond was the first.

Unstoppable!

Lance's victory made newspaper headlines around the world. It wasn't just a story about cycling. It was a story about beating the odds and not giving up. It was a story that gave hope to people fighting cancer everywhere.

Fans cheer on Lance

In the history of the Tour de France, no other rider has won more than five times.

It was also a story that didn't end. Over the next six years, Lance continued to do the impossible. He kept riding in the Tour de France, pedaling mile after **brutal** mile, and coming in first each time.

No other rider could catch Lance. No other rider could come close. In July 2005, Lance Armstrong **retired** as the winner of seven straight Tours!

Lance accepts his seventh Tour de France trophy in 2005. His son, Luke, and his twin daughters, Isabelle and Grace, are with him.

Just the Facts

More About Lance Armstrong and the Tour de France

★ **Counting Calories**—It takes a lot of energy to ride the Tour de France. On tough days, cyclists may burn 10,000 calories, four times as many as someone lounging around the house. Riders need to eat very big meals when each day's stage is done.

★ **Lance Loves Yellow**—Why did Lance often wear yellow in the Tour de France? The reason is because he was frequently in the lead. The yellow jersey is a special privilege for the rider in first place. There are other jerseys, too. The polka dot jersey goes to the fastest rider in the mountains. The green jersey goes to the best **sprinter**. The white jersey is for the best young rider.

Timeline

This timeline shows some important events in Lance Armstrong's life and career.

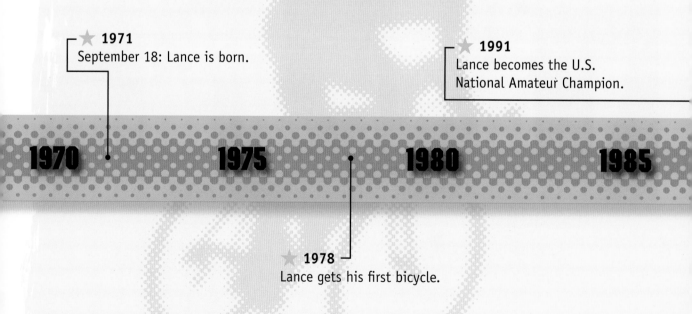

★ **1971**
September 18: Lance is born.

★ **1991**
Lance becomes the U.S.
National Amateur Champion.

1970   1975   1980   1985

★ **1978**
Lance gets his first bicycle.

★ **The Bike**—To ride the toughest race, cyclists need a special bike. Here's a look at Lance's ride.

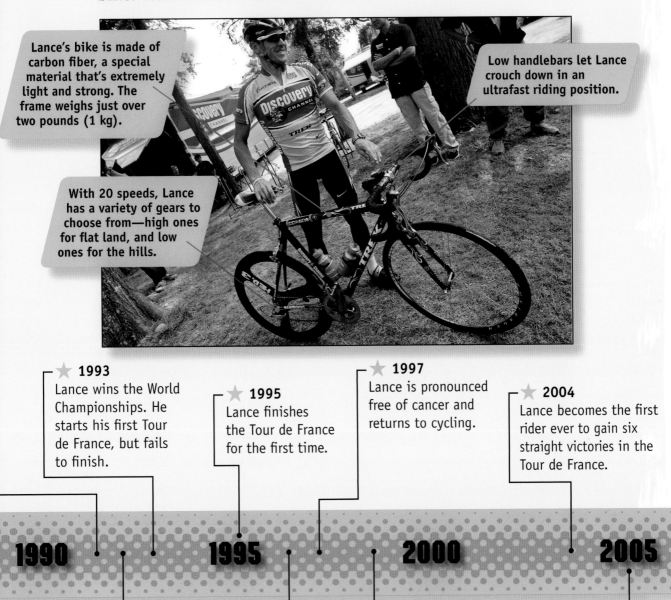

Lance's bike is made of carbon fiber, a special material that's extremely light and strong. The frame weighs just over two pounds (1 kg).

Low handlebars let Lance crouch down in an ultrafast riding position.

With 20 speeds, Lance has a variety of gears to choose from—high ones for flat land, and low ones for the hills.

★ **1993**
Lance wins the World Championships. He starts his first Tour de France, but fails to finish.

★ **1995**
Lance finishes the Tour de France for the first time.

★ **1997**
Lance is pronounced free of cancer and returns to cycling.

★ **2004**
Lance becomes the first rider ever to gain six straight victories in the Tour de France.

1990   **1995**   **2000**   **2005**

★ **1992**
Lance turns pro, finishing last in his first race

★ **1996**
Lance is diagnosed with cancer and begins treatment.

★ **1999**
Lance wins the Tour de France for the first time.

★ **2005**
Lance wins a record seventh Tour de France and retires from cycling.

Glossary

amateur (AM-uh-chur) athletes who are not professional, who don't receive money for performing

brutal (BROO-tuhl) extremely tough or difficult

compete (kuhm-PEET) to try as hard as possible in order to win

conserving (kuhn-SURV-ing) saving; storing up

depressing (di-PRES-ing) saddening; making you feel gloomy

determination (di-ter-min-AY-shun) the desire to complete the task you have decided to take on

hurtling (HUR-tuhl-ing) moving at great speed

individual (*in*-duh-VIJ-oo-uhl) single; separate

laps (LAPS) completed trips around a track or course

pressure (PRESH-ur) heavy burden; strain

professional (pruh-FESH-uh-nuhl) getting paid to do something rather than just doing it for fun; pro

retired (ri-TYE-urd) stopped working forever, usually because of age

rugged (RUHG-id) rough; jagged

sprinter (SPRINT-ur) a person who rides fast for a short distance

strategy (STRAT-uh-jee) careful and clever plan for winning

Tour de France (TOOR DUH FRANS) a three-week-long bicycle race held in France each year

treatments (TREET-mintz) medical remedies such as drugs or operations to bring about a cure

will (WIL) the ability to complete a desired task; strong purpose

Bibliography

Armstrong, Lance. *It's Not About the Bike: My Journey Back to Life.* New York: Penguin (2000).

Coyle, Daniel. *Lance Armstrong's War.* New York: HarperCollins (2005).

Wheatcroft, Geoffrey. Le Tour: *A History of the Tour de France.* London: Simon & Schuster UK Ltd (2003).

Wilcockson, John. *23 Days in July: Inside Lance Armstrong's Record-Breaking Tour de France Victory.* New York: Da Capo Press (2005).

Read More

Armstrong, Kristin. *Lance Armstrong: The Race of His Life.* New York: Grosset & Dunlap (2000).

Armstrong, Lance. *Lance Armstrong: Images of a Champion.* New York: Rodale (2004).

Hautzig, David. *1,000 Miles in 12 Days: Pro Cyclists on Tour.* New York: Orchard Books (1995).

Kramer, Barbara. *Lance Armstrong: Determined to Beat the Odds.* Berkeley Heights, NJ: Enslow (2005).

Learn More Online

Visit these Web sites to learn more about cycling, Lance Armstrong, and the Tour de France:

team.discovery.com/

www.lancearmstrong.com/

www.olntv.com/gallery

www.sikids.com/news/features/tourdefrance05/index.html

Index

About the Author

Michael Sandler lives in Brooklyn, New York. He has written numerous books on sports for children and young adults. His two children, Laszlo and Asha, are not quite old enough to read them yet.